My Camel Wants To Be a Unicorn

Written by
Julia Inserro

Designed and Illustrated by
Tanja Varcelija

W9-BMN-323

I think my camel wants
to be a **unicorn**.

My little sister had a birthday party.

It was unicorn-themed and my
camel has not been right ever since.

Was it because the unicorn gifts were so exciting? Was it the party hats everyone was wearing? Maybe she ate too many unicorn cupcakes?

I'm not sure, but it's clear to me my camel wants to be a unicorn.

I caught her trying to wear one
of the party hats as a horn.
It kept slipping down and covering her eyes.

"I love you the way you are," I told her.
"You are the best camel I have ever had."
But my camel was distracted.

She tried to make a horn out of
a paper towel tube and a lot of tape.

I tried to cheer her up
and took her on a rollercoaster.
She barely offered a "Wheee!"

I found her staring longingly
into the ice cream shop, so
I thought she wanted her favorite alfalfa cone.
She ate the ice cream
but then stuck the cone on her head!

We went to the beach, but she
didn't want to help me build a sandcastle.
Things were getting serious!
I needed my happy camel back!

We visited the library,
but she didn't even want to stay for story time.

We tried star gazing one night,
but she couldn't stop wiggling.

We got out the paddling pool,
but she wouldn't splash at all.

I was getting worried.
I took her to the doctor.

The doc had her touch her toes, checked her eyes, even had her stick out her tongue. Everything was normal.
And yet, I had one mopey camel.

One day we went
for a walk in the woods.
While walking, I asked,
"Why do you want to be a unicorn?
Camels have a big furry hump,
unicorns only have a horn."
But she didn't answer.

I kept walking and then
realized I was alone.
Where was my camel?

"There you are!" I said.
I suddenly understood what she actually
wanted, and I knew how I could help her!

As we raced home,
I told her my idea.
She loved it!

She helped me dig through
our garden tools to find my toy rake.
Then we went through the ribbon bin.
She chose a shiny purple.

After a few adjustments, it was perfect!

My camel is now the happiest camel on the block.
She never wanted to be a unicorn.
She just wanted a horn
so she could scratch her itch.
She's definitely the best camel ever!

Dromedary camels
have one hump.
They live in
the Middle East and Africa.
They love alfalfa ice cream
and rollercoasters.

Bactrian camels
have two humps.
They live in Asia.
They are furrier and have
no sense of humor.

Dedicated to my three magic beans
L, M & N, and all the
beloved camels we see every day.

Get your FREE activity book at www.juliainserro.com

Author: Julia Inserro
Illustrator: Tanja Varcelija
Printed in the United States of America
First Printing, 2019
ISBN 978-1-947891-05-0

Made in the USA
San Bernardino, CA
13 April 2020